BODY INFERNO

SHARRAS WHITE

BODY INFERNO

Acknowledgment

First and foremost, I would like to thank God. None of this would be possible without the strength and wisdom He has granted me.

I would like to thank my mother, Dianne. I would not have become the strong individual that I am today without her. I would also like to extend a special thank you to the people that are very close to me: Donell, Michael, Sheila and Terrell. I love you with all my heart.

To the people in my life that have inspired me: Shelley, Kailer, Kenneth, Tameka, Angela, Devon and Aubrey. May your inspiration continue to drive me.

You all know who you are and how much you mean to me. You have been an extreme force in my life and my project. Thank you for your support and friendship. My gratitude towards you is unending. No one achieves success without the help of others. The wise and confident acknowledge this with thankfulness. Know that you have all of my love, unconditionally.

Last but not least, to my future offspring: I do this for you and your future children.

My success in this project is a result of my devotion to the love I have for all of you.

Table of Contents

NO RING

Cold hearted

Yes cold hearted, I've become

The one before you already said that

Yes, I already know what you are about to say

So frustrated with men

I'm thinking about becoming gay

By the way, where is your ring at?

That was rhetorical

No need to answer that

The light tan around your ring finger is there!

Just because you take your wedding ring off

Doesn't mean your wife will disappear

You claim there are problems at home

And the marriage is on the rocks

Looking at me seductively

While you take another shot of Cîroc®

I can tell you're undressing me with your eyes

Beyond my control

I start to feel

A warm sensation between my thighs

I know this is wrong, but it feels so right

Leaving my morals at the bar

Cause I know we're gonna fuck tonight

I follow you to the bathroom stalls

Sixteen miss calls!

I bet it's your wife

Sliding in raw

You better pullout

I'm not ready to create life

Swimming in my loving

You can feel it

It's as hot as an oven

Pounding my body up against the wall

You whisper in my ear,

"Hey, my name is Paul"

I just met you

I don't know your number

Let alone your government

Or plan to see you after tonight

I feel regret

But I might as well finish, right?

Riding and straddling your body

Hot sex

God damn this feels better than a Molly

We've climaxed

And start to fix our clothes

I feel a charlie horse in my leg

All the way to my toes

"Last call"

It's late I just heard the bartender shout

No need to speak, I know you gotta head out

Married men are bad news

The wife always finds the dirt

Be careful when you get home

You have red lipstick on your shirt

TRUTH

I wanted to sing, but my vocal cords didn't work

I wanted to write songs, but he wanted to fuck me first

So I put my thoughts in a book

I know these words sound just like a pop song or an

R&B hook

Just late night thoughts filled with heavy breathing

Misconception from loving words and French kissing

Things men promised but I'm still missing

The reason for the lack of trust

Is the fact that lust

Is out in the open

Everywhere and love is hidden

Somewhere...

But don't be mad

Don't change your heart

Don't change your morals

And start fucking in the dark

Love is possible in this day and age

It's just much harder to weave through

The bullshit that keeps coming our way

SOCIAL NETWORK

I wish I were your social network

I would see and hear from you every day

Share all your flaws

Keep all your secrets

And love everything

CYBER SPACE

Text me

Call me

E-mail me

Wonderful things

I keep looking

At your naughty words

And impressive photos

While I sing

Sing to myself

About freaky things

Wanting you so badly

But you're too far away from me

So my fingers

And imagination

Will invite moisture

In between my thighs

Washing this feeling away

Will never work

Even if I showered a 1000 times

Photos and written words

Enhanced our bond

My device

Has aided me in this love affair

I carry my charger everywhere

Phone settings programmed

So my notifications

Are on constant alert

Mind fucking me

Without your physical presence

You entice me

And hug my soul with your words

That's why I know what you like

We have exhausted

All the words in the alphabet

There's nothing left to say

So when we meet

Body language

Is the only communication we need

I just want to see you

Touch you

While I massage my face

In your sweet water

My cheeks, lips and forehead

All hydrated

Paint me

Yes, that liquid

Provides my skin

With vitamin E

Licking your thighs and belly

Giving your manhood

The signal that it needs

As silent screams

And strong moans fill the room

Letting him know it's time

Tickling the tip with my tongue

Saliva hangs form every end

Like a spider from its web

You become stronger

As pre-cum flows out

I know he is ready

To go again and again

Reminding you

Of the past events

We've messaged

In recent months

My cyber lover

I hope this high never ends

ODD NUMBERS

17 missed calls

53 texts

97 e-mails

But none from you

Seeking your attention

Remembering our time

When I was eager

To touch you with passion

I had left my mothers guidance

At the front door

Gazing at your silhouette

In the dim light

Like a lion in heat

Pondering about this surprise

Like a belated present I hadn't received

Anxious to open

But this gift

Has no shiny wrapping paper

Or red bows

Instead it's decorated

With black buttons

And cotton strings

Your nod is the confirmation

That it's my turn

Yes, my turn to see

Taste, smell, and feel you

I rush to the buttons

On your virgin cotton shirt

Love is what I ask for

But sex is the only guarantee

The strokes are so passionate

Forces of your manhood enters

Oh wow, it feels like love

It looks like love

But I know

It's just a figment of my imagination

The fairytale that Disney lied about

You leave me with a smile

Promising a text within the hour

But I know

I know it's over

Before it has began

Your lifestyle

Has controlled your character,

Morals, and judgment

Our moment together

Will be ever lasting in my memory

I'll see you once again

And say hello with a smile

Knowing that once upon a time

Your head was between my thighs

17 missed calls

53 texts

97 e-mails

But none from you

TELL ME

Tell me

All the right things

I want you to tell me

How sorry and regretful you are

Tell me

How no one has filled that void

Tell me

It pains you thinking about me every second of the day

Tell me

How this is one big mess

And your hurtful actions

Are the result of your insecurities getting the best of you

Tell me!!!

That all you speak of is me

And you lose sleep at night

Wondering whom I'm with

And where I might be

Tell me that!!!

You haven't been the same

And your world is shattered

Tell me that you truly miss

Truly Miss me

Tell me please that you miss me!

HER

We haven't had sex in months

Subscribing to Pornhub for 3 months

You're coming home late every night

I bite my tongue

Trying not to start another fight

Getting our son ready for bed early

So I can have some pleasure

Masturbating to movies

Titled "Bang Bros Seek Lost Treasure"

I have found another to touch me

A passion mark on my breast

I pray you won't notice or see

We were only meeting up to gossip

And grab a cup of coffee

I told her about us

And how much we fuss

A shoulder to cry on

Gave me cherry lips to ride on

I screamed no in my mind

But I continued to motion my body

On her face and grind

I came so many times

I lost count

Wetness all over the couch

A ridiculous amount

I never knew I could feel this kind of sensation

Without having a male's penetration

She whispered eating

Isn't cheating

Asked me to come with her and start a new life

No longer do I want to be a housewife

I have to leave you and my son!

I want her in my life

You and I are done

A family is not in the cards for me

That was so hard to say

I just married you because the church

Said it was the only way

Please raise our son

To be all he can be

You can have full custody

All I need is her tongue licking my body

Bags packed by the front door

Stop begging me

I don't want this life anymore

I have to go

It's two-thirty and my flights leaves at four

I've been calling her all day

But she hasn't responded

Finally she sends a text

"Stop calling, I'm not gay!"

CATCH 22

We are not in love

But I stay

Because he pays the bills

Apartment in Manhattan

And shopping in Beverly Hills

He has other women

I feel it in my gut

Texting on his iPhone

But always pressing the top button

When I look up

He only request sex

Every other month

Just to make sure it's his

So the pussy is kept

Tight and untouched

I guess that's why

He claims he loves me so much

I can't complain

Because when we go out

We never go Dutch

Platinum Amex

No questions necessary

About the card being mine

No ID required

They just say

"Miss please sign your name above the dotted line"

Come on, lady

You know this card isn't mine

But this is my own fault

Wanting things too quickly

Not willing to work harder

But the independent women I know

Are lonely

Lonely as hell

Buying dildos

Trying to bust a nut

They have it all

Except a phone call

A man with power

Needs a woman at his beck and call

I won his heart

Because she was too busy

With her conference calls

While she studied for the Bar

I was on the private jet to Madagascar

A man with a nine to five

Is fine and dandy

But when they see a girl like me

They ask "why not me"

These women look

With evil stares

I know what they're thinking

"Life's not fair"

360

I use to see you everyday

But now that's limited by the circumstances

Thinking about how things

Have become a total 360

I'm so hurt

Feeling like someone ripped out my heart

And buried it in the dirt

Trying to separate the emotional

From the physical

Love letters you wrote to me and her

Are identical

You've turn your back on me

Not a call, not a text

Why won't you respond?

Second guessing your intentions

You've put me in time out

This feels like detention

Treating me like a problem child

Your consistency and attentiveness

Have come to an end

A bitter woman once told me never to trust men

She was once like me

Until someone like you broke her heart

So now the cycle starts

I will never feel

I promised myself

I can't believe you've left me

All by myself

Searching for answers

Has only lead to confusion

I can't let go

Telling myself I'm settling

Wanting someone who wants me

And just me alone

But hey, he has it all

Another purse to hide my hurt

Another bracelet to shine in my darkest hour

I turned on TMZ

You two were in the hotel shower

My dignity, I have lost

I'll give you time to make up something false

Clear as day but you'll tell me it's a lie

Holding the phone to my ear

All I can do is cry

This is what happens

When you're in love with a rock star

Now I'm regretting not studying for the Bar

SHAME

I hate this part

Entering the glass doors

Then approaching the front desk

This is the "Walk of Shame"

Checking in

Room number and alias name

We lie to our love ones

Just for this temporary high

You're working late

So I take a shower and wait

You're a star

Yet you become human

You become mine

Forget the rules of the love game

Because I have no shame

No shame in my words

No shame in my actions

Stealing moments

After this night you'll start living again

But I'll be stuck in time

For this body I yearn for is not mine

Yet for some reason when your inside me

I feel like a bride

You're my something borrowed

And I'm your something blue

Thinking to myself

That I'll never find someone new

Using your body to pleasure mine

Is a gift and a curse

Tomorrow you'll send your assistant

Out to purchase another Hermès purse

That won't solve a thing

I just want you around

I don't want anything

You're always on my mind

The dates during the day

Are just activities to occupy my brain

I swear, I feel silly

I must be insane

Making love to someone

Who wears a tattoo of another

Crying in silence

I can't tell a soul

Not even my mother

Let's be honest

I'm making love to myself

While we're having sex

I'm so ashamed

But I am the only one to blame

I'm done!!

I keep telling myself

I'm done!!!

Please God!

Let me be done!

Eighty-one thousand in the bank

But I feel like a homeless bum

Demoralized

I'm numb

Slitting my wrist

Feeling no pain

I saw you two together

In public side by side

Why couldn't you love me?

My last thoughts before suicide

TIME

I pray that I'll find true love

And never run out of time

Never to settle for the moments

Settle for the person that I only like

I pray I'll get that two-way street

I pray I'll never have learn to love

While my true love is with another

Because of this thing called life

We tend to settle

For the ones who makes sense

And stop believing in love

When we get older

The people we tried to impress won't matter

But the feeling of regret

Will forever burn inside

Life may be short but true love is forever

I pray I'll find true love and not run out of time

GONE

To know he is no longer here

Has shattered my soul

The day of his funeral

I walk up the concrete steps

I hear people

Yes, they're family

But to me, they are just people

Annoying human beings

Giving me condolences

Statements such as,

"It's Gods time with him"

"God makes no mistakes"

"The Lord has sent for his angel"

Fuck you!

Fuck you

You know nothing

About "Him"

"God"

"The Lord"

He worshiped God

Day and night

Praying and singing His gospel

I sat in that room

And watched him in pain

Watched him struggle

To take a single breath

No visits,

No phone calls from anyone

But you did send a get-well text

You rather spend your time

Updating photos and comments online

You've come here

To show love for a dead person

Not him

Cause you were too busy

To see him alive

Your love and support

Is a mask of guilt and fear

Fear of karma

Fear that one day

You will be abandoned

By your love ones

You speak of God

While taking photos

And posting on your timeline

About sudden sadness

You couldn't wait

To wear your designer labeled

Black on black, huh?

I want to cremate all of you alive

So you can feel the pain I feel inside

The sorrow I felt

When I lost the only person who understood me

Keep talking

Keep telling me

About God's will

Cause after all

If I do light this bitch on fire

God will save you, right?

CHAMP

After I cum I rather not be touched

It's not me being rude

I just don't love you that much

There is a thin line and I rather not cross it

Because disappointment

Always comes when

I start to look forward to it

Forward to phone calls

Forward to the good morning texts

I look back and I start to believe

It was just sex

So after I cum I rather not be touched

Just give me sec

It's only sex

Because the formalities

We haven't done

We have started from the end

Exposing everything

Before learning anything

Anything about each other

No, the first thought

Was when could we fuck one another

Avoiding your lips

Giving you clues to focus lower

Kissing kept at a minimum

Because I know

This is the fastest way

To be love sprung

Lift my legs

Just use your tongue

Sliding my cheeks

Knock me out

Bust a nut

Change in the rules

Just keep the hits below the belt

Kissing in the mouth

Is only going to make my heart melt

Remember after I cum

I rather not be touched

PERFECT

Perfect in every way

I'm everything you ever wanted

But unfortunately

Your dreams were delayed

You aren't where you wanted be in life

Falling into my shadow was never my intention

You frown upon my accomplishments

Wishing it were you they applaud

Seeking attention

Constantly needing a reminder

Of your worth by many voices

But I was your number one fan

My praises

Should have been all you needed

Guess that wasn't enough

You desired to be seen first

And last in a crowded room

Wanted to be adored

In the eyes of nobodies

To feel like you were somebody

I see you walking with her

Wondering to yourself

Why every time you two make love

All you see are visions of me

But once upon a time

You were my perfect

Perfect in every way

TEAM

Every morning

I have to consciously stop my brain

From thinking about you

And remind my heart

Not to love you

A crazy lady I've become

Cause you put that thing on me

And drove me insane

Daily activities distract my brain

But late at night the fact remains

I miss you

Can you hear what I'm saying?

I miss you

No more bullshit

No more games

Can you please just stop

Fucking them silly dames

I really miss you

I wish you could be tamed

I thought I could have satisfied

Your sexual appetite

But you don't come home

To me every night

So the fact remains

You say you miss me

But your actions don't speak the same

I heard you telling the world

You have your women on lock

And all of them go crazy

After you introduce them to your cock

Bragging and talking trash

Like the guys on First Take

About the love we make?

You don't miss me

At least that's not how it seems

It's quite clear

I'm just another bad bitch on your team

CAFFEINE

My coffee cup

The smell of you

Just wakes me up

Visions of you in my mind

I talk to myself

Talking to you all the time

Can I just kiss your face?

Touch that thing below your waist?

I swear it's really innocent

So tell me

Tell me

Your final answer

I swear my kitty

Is the correct answer

Cold and heartless

I hear you are a very busy man

Traveling all around the world

And have many women

In the palm of your hand

But baby, my coffee cup

My coffee cup

I swear you'll feel

Like you've won a million bucks

Speak of what you need

And you will receive

Making you love sprung

Is something I'm determine to achieve

I'll serve you

Whatever the deed

How much of my sugar

And honey do you need?

I want to be the woman of your dreams

Not just one of many players on your team

My coffee cup

Just give me a chance

I'll wake your heart up

BFFs

At night I touch myself

And think of you

Visions of your lower body

Wrestling inside me

While I shower your manhood

With my moistness

Gasping for air

Every thrust of your body

Gives me oxygen

I breathe you

Yes, I breathe you

I feel like I'm floating

They call this a sin

I call this heaven on earth

Wanting you to never stop

And to be in this moment forever

Even though I know

We're not technically together

Holding back emotions

Because I wasn't sure of yours

Maybe I should have

Maybe I could have

Questions and answers

When I start to forget you

Suddenly, you reappear

Your lips speak of love

And give me hope

That a committed relationship is near

Who am I kidding?

Your feelings for me don't exist

I thought I was strong enough for this

Waited on your phone call

But it never came

Friends with benefits

A terrible part of the love game

REGRET

Thinking about you everyday

I wonder how long it's going to take

To get over you

How long it's going to take

For me to let go

Looking down at the club's floor

Ignoring when others approach

Trying to take your place

Promising me the world

And how different

They would love me

If given the chance

But I don't want them

I'm just tired of trying

So tired of giving

My time

Over and over again

I curse myself

For giving mind and soul

Taking my body

Was just a task

To satisfy my needed high

That's not the issue

But the intimacy

Is what pains my heart

The kisses

The hugs

The texts

The calls

I didn't see this coming

Falling in love

Can happen

In the blink of an eye

Falling out of love

Seems to take much longer

I feel sorry for the one after you

The things he will endure

Thanks to the emotional bruises

You left on my heart

I seek answers

Only you can answer

Instead they are answered

By voices in my head

Useless advice

From friends

With their own dysfunctional relationships

Male friends who have hidden intentions

With their penises

Nothing last forever

But memories do

Memories of you and me

Laughter and smiles

Waking up in middle of the night

Wanting to hear your voice

Counting the hours

Until I see your smile

Listening to love songs

Relating all the lyrics

To our time together

Thinking about you everyday

I just want to forget you

To erase you

I regret you

SOUL

The devil knocked on my door today

The laws of attraction

Are telling me there is something approaching

Something bigger than life itself

Unfortunately these obstacles

Are pulling me in sinful directions

Please show me a sign

Bring me something so rewarding

That my enemies will cringe

To the site of my earnings

Let all my dreams come to pass

Let me be blessed with security

Let me not have to sell my soul

The devil knocks on my door everyday

And today I answered

But I did not let him in

I'm afraid I will next time

And I'll fall to his feet

For the plan that God has for me

Is taking too long

But the shame

The pressure

Of not succeeding

Is draining me

People speak of honesty

In a world of full deception

Selling our souls

Seems to be the only link

To a powerful connection

Men promise love and support

They want to give a temporary wet incentive

Love has no definition

So I can't call this lie

More like another form of deception

Someone once said,

"People attract who they are"

I guess they're right

I'm slowly becoming

The people I once judged

I knew what it meant

When he gave my left thigh a nudge

Wanting a piece of the pie

Would require a night with Mr. suit & tie

The devil knocked on my door today

Because of my faith I walked away

I'll wait on God

He will answer me one day

ALONE

I wish you were here

But you're not

Waking up in my bed

Alone has become my living grave

I pray to be in a conscious death

Just to see visions of you

Wondering if this feeling is mutual

May be the fuel to my high

Your existence has become

The reason for my intoxication

I have seen you

Felt you

And inhaled you many times

But never have I owned you

You've left me with an uncontrollable desire

Yet never satisfied

So I will always return

Knowing the ending of the story

I continue to rewind to my favorite part

Deep down inside

I'm expecting

The outcome to change

It never does

You never do

You always say

And then you go away

Your actions have lasted

More than 21 days

So this has become

A constant pattern

That may never change

You've learned

How to love me

And I've accepted

Your offer

Time and time again

Needing more

But too afraid to ask

Not wanting to risk

You never existing in my reality

I wish you were here

But you're not

MIND OVER MATTER

I pretended it was you

The heart loves

But my body does what it wants to

Guess you heard

Cause now you call

I pretended it was you

The heart loves

But my body just does what it wants to

If you would have just answered one of my 26 texts

Now you pretend

Pretend with someone else

That it's me

Shame, the thrill

The chase was a camouflage

Now you see

Now you're the one in agony

But it's too late

I no longer pretend

My heart doesn't remember you

Because I've found ecstasy

I've found a sexual beast

And most importantly

Someone who loves me

ANTHEM

Promiscuous thoughts

In my head

I wanna make you feel great

Taking out all of your inner frustrations

Completely taking them away

My tongue's slurps translate:

"I need you please, please"

As you release into my mouth

I feel your warm mixture down my throat

Standing with my knees

I pledge allegiance to your body

I've gained a six sense

And it has taken over my mind

As well as my heart

Using your body

Yes, indeed but needing your heart

You've become a new found creed

And the sounds of our bodies

In motion is a sweet gospel

Attacking every inch of your anatomy

With my lips leaving you

In a conscious wet dream

You take over and promise

To pleasure me the same

As I've done

But don't you understand?

Just seeing your reaction

To my sinful actions

Has satisfied me

Just enough

So unorthodox

You've mind fucked me

And made me cum all on sight

Emotions are the only remedy

For gaining my love

My love demands more

Than a temporary incentive

Oh no, I want a feeling

Of a ever lasting borderline obsession

We have sex with our bodies

But we will make love with our hearts

I know it's the first date

But lets get takeout

I wanna go home

And get a head start

LONDON

Within seconds

You've become my instructor

Dictating the motion of my mouth

Loud moans fill the room

Our tongue and saliva

Are the only tools needed

Sinful actions in the dark

The bright light from your blackberry

Aids your lens to focus and see

Phone notifications go unanswered

Cause we're obviously in heat

Kissing and stroking your manhood

While you smack and choke me

Following every verbal and physical command

Your dick throbs

I think this thing

Has its own brain and heart beat

It speaks to me

You grasp my neck tightly

And instruct me

On how to turn my head in every direction

So I can successfully please

You pick up speed

And pump and hump my mouth vigorously

Flatting my tongue

Making it eventually disappear

So you slide down my throat effortlessly

Sucking and spitting on each others body parts

This is mind blowing

It's insane

Feeling the adrenaline Danica felt in the fast lane

Every time my lips release you

A pool of wetness remains

Yours, mine

Just a pool of cum

Spit and more cum

You just went down there

I didn't see you do a "check"

You just believed in me

Knowing I'd be just like water

Fragrant free

My clit rides your tongue

Legs shake

Great stamina

No need for a break

Over and over we take turns

Cause 69 is too intense for me

But I'll master that sooner than later

Professor

Yes, indeed

Feasting all night

The oral exchange

The ultimate feast

THANK YOU

I love that I let you go

Cause I started

Wanting to do things out of spite

Like hurting you

Like you hurt me

Things like waiting until you took a nap

And killing your ass

Like the bitches on a episode of Snapped

No, I'm going let it go and relax

I love that I let you go

Cause I started

Wanting to do things out of spite

Like hurting you

Like you hurt me

Thank you